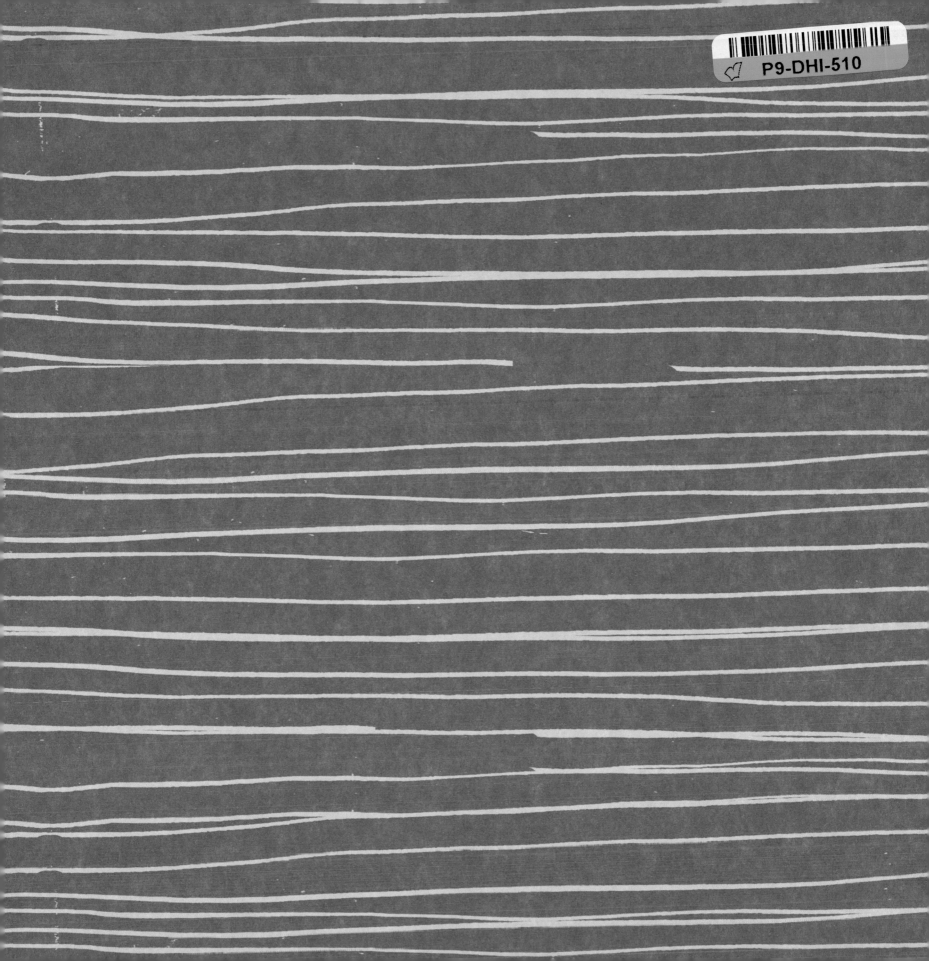

To my dad, Amos. You get what you get . . .
and I'm so thankful I got you. -jg

 is published by
Picture Window Books, A Capstone Imprint
1710 Roe Crest Drive
North Mankato, Minnesota 56003
www.capstonepub.com

Library of Congress Cataloging-in-Publication data is
available on the Library of Congress website.

ISBN: 978-1-4048-6794-9 (library binding)
ISBN: 978-1-4795-2157-9 (paper over board)

Designer: Hilary Wacholz

Printed in the United States of America in North Mankato, Minnesota.
042017   010492R

YOU GET WHAT YOU GET

by Julie Gassman   illustrated by Sarah Horne

Melvin did not deal well
with disappointment.

If his cookie had half as many chocolate chips as his sister's, LOOK OUT!

If he lost his turn during a game,
STAND BACK!

And if he didn't get exactly what he wanted...

well, you know...

"Sorry, Melvin, they were out of dinosaur backpacks."

No, Melvin did **NOT** deal well with disappointment.

And this is why he **HATED** his teacher's favorite rule.

Because of this rule, Melvin could not throw a fit if he had to use crayons instead of markers.

He could not throw a fit if he ended up last in line.

He couldn't even throw a fit if his napkin was pink instead of green.

"Oh, well," mumbled Melvin, "at least I can still throw a fit at home. My family doesn't know a thing about that **TERRIBLE** rule."

But that night when it was Melvin's turn to choose the movie, things changed. As soon as he'd chosen *Dinosaur Rumble*, his sister stomped her foot and whined,

"But I want to watch
A Pony Called Trouble!"

"**TOO BAD!** You get what you get,
and you don't throw a fit," said Melvin.

Everyone stopped and looked at Melvin.

"What did you say?" asked Dad.

"You get what you get, and you
don't throw a fit," repeated Melvin.

"So if your cookie only has a few chocolate chips,
you shouldn't throw a fit?" asked his sister.

"And if you lose a turn during a game,
you shouldn't throw a fit?" asked his dad.

"And if the dinosaur backpacks are all sold out, you should be happy with the robot one, and you absolutely should not throw a fit?" asked his mom.

Melvin gulped. There was no way to take it back.

EVERYONE KNEW.

"Well, I mean, at school you shouldn't throw a fit, 'cause that's the rule. But at home, you can," he said.

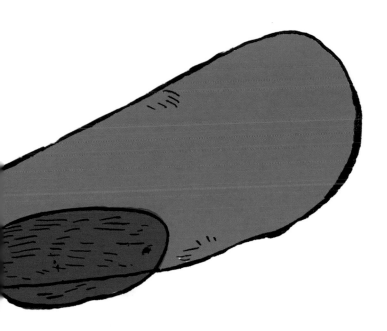

"I think that sounds like a good rule for at home, too," said Dad.

"I agree!" said Mom.

"Home and school, that's the rule!" his sister chanted.

Melvin wanted to **CRY.**

He wanted to **SHOUT.**

He wanted to lie down on the ground and **THROW** his arms and legs about.

But he didn't.

After all, you get what you get,
and you don't throw a fit.

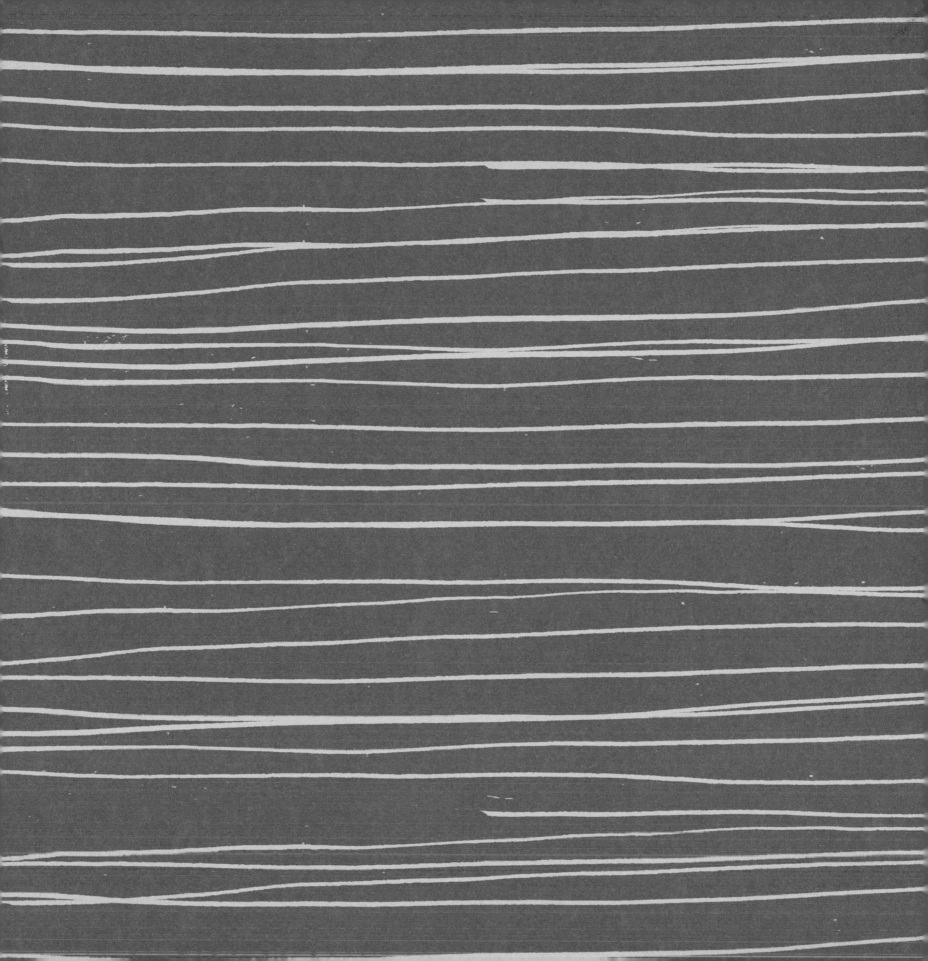

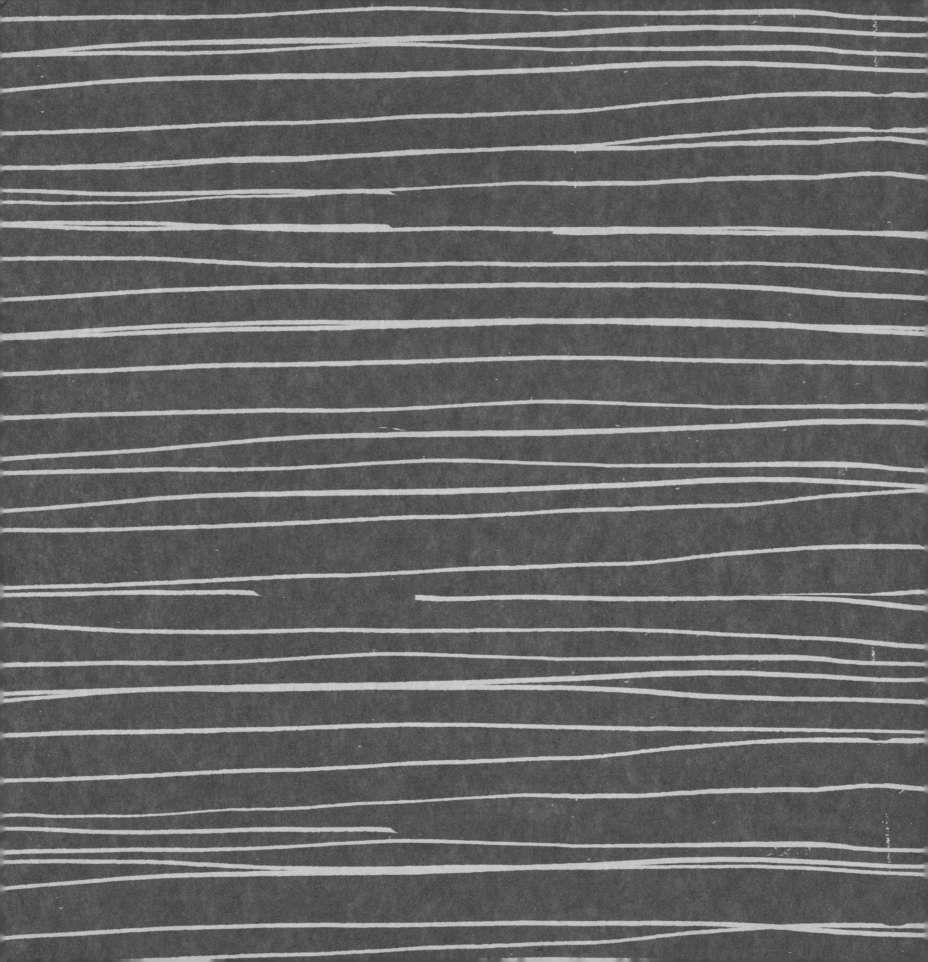